LETTER TOWN

BY **DARREN FARRELL**

Scholastic Inc.

For Heather, Celia, Jessica,
Joo-Young, and Patti Ann

Copyright © 2018 by Darren Farrell

All rights reserved. Published by Scholastic Inc., *Publishers since 1920*. SCHOLASTIC and associated logos are trademarks and/or registered trademarks of Scholastic Inc.

The publisher does not have any control over and does not assume any responsibility for author or third-party websites or their content.

No part of this publication may be reproduced, stored in a retrieval system, or transmitted in any form or by any means, electronic, mechanical, photocopying, recording, or otherwise, without written permission of the publisher. For information regarding permission, write to Scholastic Inc., Attention: Permissions Department, 557 Broadway, New York, NY 10012.

This book is a work of fiction. Names, characters, places, and incidents are either the product of the author's imagination or are used fictitiously, and any resemblance to actual persons, living or dead, business establishments, events, or locales is entirely coincidental.

ISBN 978-1-338-31588-2

10 9 8 7 6 5 4 3 2 1 • 18 19 20 21 22

Printed in the U.S.A. 169 • First printing 2018
The illustrations for this book were done using a collection of Japanese and Korean brush pens, and colored in Adobe Photoshop.
The text type was set in Johann • The display type was hand lettered.
Book design by Jess Tice-Gilbert

Excuse me, friend, have you yet
seen the home of the alphabet?
Come with me, I'll show you around
this lovely place called Letter Town.

Folks call me Bus Driver B.
I'll drive us all from A to Z.

We'll take a tour down every street
and see which letters we can meet.

 Do you see nine A's at work and play?
We'll pick one up and take her away.

All aboard, A! What do I see?
I wonder who that R might be?

 B

Loads of B's enjoy the beach.
Do you know the name of each?

All aboard, B! What do I see?
Thanks for the bagels, Baker B!

C

Near the circus, we'll stop to get
Cowboy C and a D who's all wet.

All aboard, C and D! What do I see?
Who's being followed by Detective D?

How many E's and F's are there out enjoying the country air?

All aboard, E and F! What do I see?
Who do you think our next letter will be?

Time for gas, watch me pull in
next to a G with a giant grin.

All aboard, G! What do I see?
One G holds something pretty stinky.

H

Right on time, with no delay,
Here come the H's on holiday!

All aboard, H! What do I see?
This H has a hug for everybody.

Across the bridge, we'll pick up three
letters waiting patiently.

All aboard, I, J, K! What do I see?
Where on earth is Detective D?

K

Take a look, can you guess who
on this street has a book for you?

All aboard, L! What do I see?
Shh, let's read our books quietly.

M

Magician M, where did he go?
POOF! He's sitting near the window.

All aboard, **M**! What do I see?
Three Monster M's from a movie.

Has anyone seen Ninja N?
Will Opera O's song ever end?

All aboard, N and O! What do I see?
Hurry up, you guys, it's time to get P!

Sorry I'm late, P and Q!
Did you think I had forgotten you?

All aboard, P and Q! What do I see?
Let's order a pizza with pepperoni!

R Here comes an R with a black mask.
Who could he be? I'm afraid to ask.

All aboard, R! What do I see?
Is R a member of the royalty?

Up on the roof comes a HO, HO, HO.
Who is that, do you know, know, know?

All aboard, S! What do I see?
S thinks R has been naughty.

T

Hear that sound that makes us bop?
It's Tuba T – let's make a stop!

All aboard, T! What do I see?
Who's that being pulled by Tow Truck T?

Let's pick up a famous U and V
at Letter Town University.

All aboard, U and V! What do I see?
Uh-oh, good-bye, Detective D!

Watch all ten little W's glide,
down the whirling waterslide.

All aboard, W! What do I see?
Who's left to get? I have seats for three.

X

Xtreme Sports X jumps right on in,
over the Yo-Yo Champion.

Y

And here's Zookeeper Z to make things right,
by bringing his zebra home for the night.

"Make room for me!" huffs Detective D.
"There's someone on board I need to see."

"What about us?" whines the rest of the zoo.
"We'd like to go home with the Zookeeper, too!"

All aboard, y'all! What do I see?
The bus is jam-packed! Hang on tightly!

Howling! Yowling! Scowling! Nonstop.
What will happen? Will the bus pop?

Phew, we made it safe and sound.

Beep! Beep! LAST STOP IN LETTER TOWN!

Everybody home, one by one.
Good-bye, B. Good-bye, sun.

Nobody on board. What do I see?
"Good night, little bus," whispers B.

Meanwhile, off go D and R for a stroll,
to give back everything that sneaky R stole.